Spring came to the woods
and Brown Bear woke
from his winter sleep.
He wanted to climb a tree
to see the rest of the woods,
but that was impossible.
Brown Bear had hurt his leg
when it got caught in a trap.

3

4

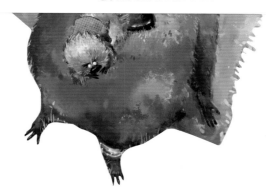

2

Sitting on the riverbank,
Brown Bear watched the beavers.
How he wished that he could swim!
But that was also impossible
because of his leg.
He cried, "I want to swim
and be free and strong
like all those beavers."

Sometimes he tried to imitate
the beavers' movements.

Grandfather Beaver saw him
and said, "What are you doing?"

Brown Bear blushed.
"I'm practising how to swim."

"Why are you doing that?"

Brown Bear said to him,
"I have this dream of going to the sea.
I can't walk there because I have a limp,
but I've heard that the river goes to the sea.
Maybe I can learn to swim."

Grandfather Beaver wanted to help the bear.
"If you want to swim to the ocean,
I will go with you in the summer.
It will be March soon. Let's go in July."

They made goals for March, April, May, and June
and decided on what they would do.

The goal for Brown Bear in March
was to build up physical strength.
He did 100 push-ups on the ground.
He did 100 pull-ups on a tree branch.
He lifted 100 rocks every day.

The goal in April was to swim in the pond.
At first it was hard for Brown Bear to float,
but as the days passed, he learned to swim.

The goal in May was to swim in the river.
That was more difficult.
Brown Bear thought he might drown.

Exhausted, Brown Bear crawled
out of the river and said,
"I don't think I can do it."

"Nonsense!" said Grandfather Beaver.
"This is your dream! Keep working at it.
It is never easy to realise a dream.
If it was easy, it wouldn't be worth having."

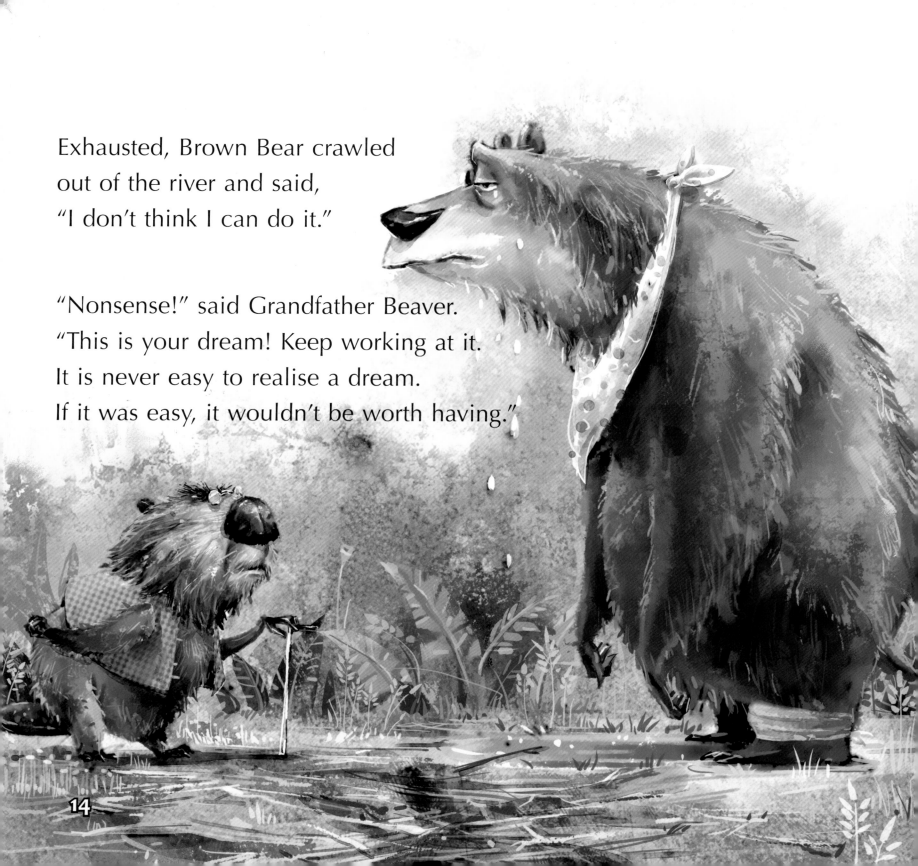

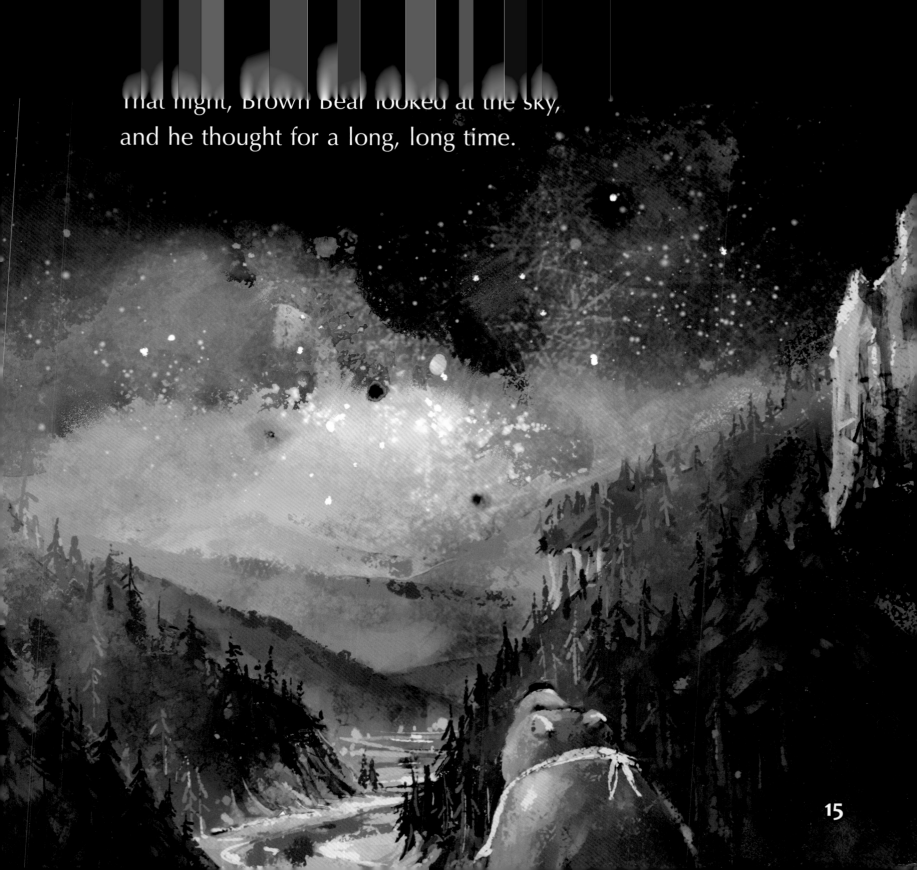

That night, Brown Bear looked at the sky,
and he thought for a long, long time.

In June, Brown Bear practised swimming
in the river. He also learned about the ocean.
He learned about big waves
and how to avoid dangerous creatures.

At last, it was July.
"Brown Bear, are you ready?"
asked Grandfather Beaver.

"Yes, I am ready," replied Brown Bear.

So Brown Bear and
Grandfather Beaver got
in the river and swam
with the current.

When the sun went down,
they slept on the riverbank.
When the sun rose,
they swam again.

19

The river grew wider.
That meant the sea was close.
But Grandfather Beaver said,
"Brown Bear, I am old
and my body is tired.
I can no longer go with you.
You must swim on by yourself."

Gathering courage,
Brown Bear swam on his own.

21

At last he came to the sea.
It was wider and more beautiful
than he had ever imagined.
"I did it! I did it!" he yelled.

22

Brown Bear went back home
and soon winter came.
He fell into a deep winter sleep.
Maybe he was dreaming up
a new dream.

25

Dear Brown Bear,

I know that it wasn't easy for you
to make your dream come true,
but you did it!
You got to the sea!
It was hard at first,
but you made goals
and kept working.
You asked for help.
You practised.
You had courage.
I am so proud of you!

Your friend,
Grandfather Beaver

big & SMALL

Original Korean text by Yun-yeong Kim
Illustrations by Kye-mahn Kim
Original Korean edition © Aram Publishing

This English edition published by big & SMALL
by arrangement with Aram Publishing
English text edited by Joy Cowley
Additional editing by Mary Lindeen
Artwork for this edition produced
in cooperation with Norwood House Press, U.S.A.
English edition © big & SMALL 2015

ISBN: 978-1-925233-91-9

Printed in Korea